A PRIZE INSIDE

A ROBOT AND RICO STORY

BY ANASTASIA SUEN
ILLUSTRATED BY MIKE LAUGHEAD

STONE ARCH BOOKS
MINNEAPOLIS   SAN DIEGO

This is **ROBOT**.
Robot has lots of
tools. He uses the
tools to help his
best friend, **Rico**.

Parents and Caregivers,

Stone Arch Readers are designed to provide enjoyable reading experiences, as well as opportunities to develop vocabulary, literacy skills, and comprehension. Here are a few ways to support your beginning reader:

- Talk with your child about the ideas addressed in the story.

- Discuss each illustration, mentioning the characters, where they are, and what they are doing.

- Read with expression, pointing to each word. You may want to read the whole story through and then revisit parts of the story to ensure that the meanings of words or phrases are understood.

- Talk about why the character did what he or she did and what your child would do in that situation.

- Help your child connect with characters and events in the story.

Remember, reading with your child should be fun, not forced. Each moment spent reading with your child is a priceless investment in his or her literacy life.

Gail Saunders-Smith, Ph.D

STONE ARCH READERS

are published by Stone Arch Books, a Capstone imprint
1710 Roe Crest Drive
North Mankato, Minnesota 56003
www.mycapstone.com

Library of Congress Cataloging-in-Publication Data
Suen, Anastasia.
    A prize inside : a Robot and Rico story / by Anastasia Suen ; illustrated by
Mike Laughead.
    p. cm. – (Stone Arch readers)
    ISBN 978-1-4342-1627-4 (library binding)
    ISBN 978-1-4342-1749-3 (pbk.)
    [1. Toys–Fiction. 2. Robots–Fiction.] I. Laughead, Mike, ill. II. Title.
PZ7.S94343Pri 2010
[E]–dc22

                                                        2009000883

Summary: Robot and Rico go to the grocery store in hopes of finding a new
Hero Cat prize in a cereal box.

Art Director: Bob Lentz
Graphic Designer: Hilary Wacholz

Reading Consultants:
Gail Saunders-Smith, Ph.D
Melinda Melton Crow, M.Ed
Laurie K. Holland, Media Specialist

Printed in the United States of America in Eau Claire, Wisconsin.
032016   009600R

 Teapot

 Wings

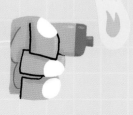 Scissors

 Fire Finger

 Special Shoes

 Roller Skates

Robot and Rico are at the grocery store.

"Do you see it?" asks Rico.

"Here's the box," says Robot.

"It's Hero Cat!" says Rico. "Can you see the prize inside, Robot?"

8

"Here's the box," says Robot.

"It's Hero Cat!" says Rico. "Can you see the prize inside, Robot?"

8

"I see the prize," says Robot.
"It is long and thin."

"Like this?" asks Rico.

"Yes," says Robot.

Rico blows a big bubble.

"I already have that," says Rico.

"Look in a new box," says Rico.

"Okay," says Robot. "I see another one."

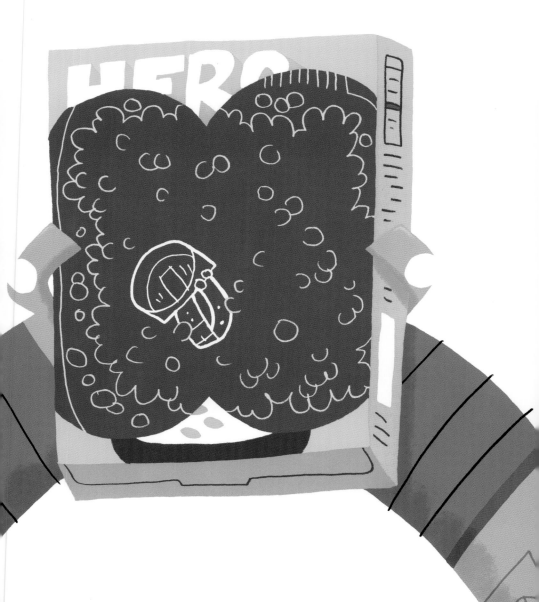

Robot holds up the box.

"I see a shiny circle," says Robot.

"Like this?" asks Rico.

"Yes," says Robot.

"I already have one," says Rico.

"Look in a new box," says Rico.

"Okay," says Robot. "I see another one."

Robot holds up the box.

"I see a long string," says Robot.

Robot looks at the box.

"It is a whistle," says Robot.

"Like this?" asks Rico.

"Wow! That's loud!" says Robot.

"Who is making all that noise?"
asks the store worker.

"Look at this mess!" he says.
"Please put all of the boxes back!"

"Yes, sir," says Robot.

Robot and Rico put all of
the boxes back.

"Can I please have one box?"
asks Rico. "I just want a Hero
Cat prize."

The man gives Rico a box.

"Enjoy your prize," he says.
"Now please leave."

Rico pays for the box.

"What is your prize?" asks Robot.

"It's a tiny square," says Rico.

"Open it," says Robot.

"It's a cape!" says Rico.
"I am Hero Cat!"

"And I am hungry," says Robot.

STORY WORDS

hero   circle   noise
prize   string   cape
bubble   whistle

Total Word Count: 273

One robot. One boy. One crazy fun friendship! Read all four Robot and Rico adventures!